ESSEX
FOLK TALES
FOR CHILDREN

ESSEX
FOLK TALES
FOR CHILDREN

JAN WILLIAMS
ILLUSTRATED BY SIMON PEECOCK

The
History
Press

First published 2018

The History Press
The Mill, Brimscombe Port
Stroud, Gloucestershire, GL5 2QG
www.thehistorypress.co.uk

© Jan Williams, 2018
Illustrations © Simon Peecock, 2018

The right of Jan Williams to be identified as the Author
of this work has been asserted in accordance with the
Copyright, Designs and Patents Act 1988.

All rights reserved. No part of this book may be reprinted
or reproduced or utilised in any form or by any electronic,
mechanical or other means, now known or hereafter invented,
including photocopying and recording, or in any information
storage or retrieval system, without the permission in writing
from the Publishers.

British Library Cataloguing in Publication Data.
A catalogue record for this book is available from the British Library.

ISBN 978 0 7509 8347 1

Typesetting and origination by The History Press
Printed and bound by CPI Group (UK) Ltd

CONTENTS

About the Author

I was born on the beautiful west coast of Wales, where there are many magic stories from cities below the waves and bells that ring out from a submerged forest. I was slow to learn to read as a child, but my mother filled my life with those stories which she told me when I had long bouts of sickness and could only lie in bed and listen. She would make up stories based on the little china figures that were dotted around the shelves of my bedroom and they became very real to me.

Luckily, at my school we were encouraged to tell stories, and later I found when

I became a teacher myself, the children I taught enjoyed the tales I had learnt in my childhood. It helped that I enjoyed travelling. I have been to Russia, America, the Ukraine, Poland, Spain and France, and I have taught in Canada, Birmingham and Maidstone. Finally, I settled in Brightlingsea in Essex, where barges and fishing smacks still float down the estuary of the River Colne.

I suddenly began to really enjoy my story-telling when I heard that excellent storyteller Taffy Thomas doing a storytelling workshop at Sidmouth, and amazingly the very next year I won Sidmouth Folk Festival Storyteller of the Year! At last I had discovered this is what I really wanted to do with my life. I wanted to be an oral storyteller, someone who told tales aloud. Luckily, I made friends with other sto-rytellers like Carl Merry and Andy Jennings, and we started the Essex Storytellers and travelled around schools, theatres, festivals, historic buildings and libraries! In that way we saw many of the places where the Essex folk tales had grown up, and collected a great deal of information from people who knew this area really well.

Jan Williams

2018

About the Illustrator

I was born into a big family in the Moulsham end of Chelmsford. My playground was the swing park of the Woolworths shop and coffee bars. The highlight of the week was Saturday morning pictures. An Essex 'Townie' in fact!

But when I hit ten all was to change. Dad's work was to take him to Colchester, and we went rural. Here I discovered our new home was the magical village of Rowhedge, 3 miles from Colchester. Here I discovered the wonder of wood and streams, gravel pits and marshes, the rhythm of tides with their wealth of birds, beasts, fish and creepy crawlies. I explored and plundered the ruined and deserted buildings of industries that put the village on the map.

Local boys taught my older brother and I the black arts of den building, firemaking and building rafts. One of our finds was an old rubbish dump. We found porcelain, kettles and bottles. I started drawing and painting as a teenager, and among my first artworks were pictures of a pale blue beautiful bottle we had found.

Our family was an arty bunch. My mother was an actor, my father was a writer and my brother was a guitarist. So it stood to reason I should be an artist. I trained for seven years at Colchester Art School, Wimbledon School of Art and the Slade. One of the teachers who helped me was Maggi Hambling. I branched out into collage, sculpture and printmaking.

I lived in London for eight years with my partner before the call of the east coast and all its treasures finally brought us to Brightlingsea.

It was good to meet Jan. Her stories intrigued me with their mix of wildlife, local history and fantasy. And I am delighted to illustrate them.

Now I have three grown-up children. And I continue to paint daily. They are sometimes my toughest critics, but just occasionally my admirers.

Simon Peecock
2018

Nursery Rhymes

The very first stories that we learn as children are usually nursery rhymes, which sometimes do not make much sense, because they have been passed down over many years and are connected with historical events that we no longer completely understand. It is quite a piece of detective work to completely understand the story, yet because they have rhyme and repeat themselves, they stay in our memories, even when we grow old! It is always interesting to find out what nursery rhymes your family can remember. Even when my mother was eighty-five years old, she still remembered the nursery rhymes of her childhood!

Sometimes we know who wrote the nursery rhymes, or sometimes they just got passed down by word of mouth from person to person over the years, with nobody saying who invented them. We can be proud of the fact that four of the best-known English nursery rhymes started in Colchester.

TWINKLE, TWINKLE LITTLE STAR

The first one I found out about was when I celebrated the anniversary of 'Twinkle, Twinkle Little Star' in the lovely gardens of Colchester Castle, in front of the pretty eighteenth-century house that is Hollytrees Museum.

BE A STAR

Twinkle, twinkle little star
How I wonder what you are!
Up above the world so high,
Like a diamond in the sky
Twinkle, twinkle little star,
How I wonder what you are!

When the blazing sun is gone;
When he nothing shines upon,
Then you show your little light,
Twinkle, twinkle all the night.
Twinkle, twinkle little star,
How I wonder what you are!

Then the traveller in the dark,
Thanks you for your tiny spark,
He could not see which way to go
If you did not twinkle so.
Twinkle, twinkle little star,
How I wonder what you are!

In the dark blue sky, you keep,
And often through my curtains peep,
For you never shut your eye,
Till the sun is in the sky,
Twinkle, twinkle little star,
How I wonder what you are!

As your bright and tiny spark,
Lights the traveller in the dark
Though I know not what you are.
Twinkle, twinkle little star
How I wonder what you are!

Now, we do know who wrote these well-loved
verses. It was a girl called Jane Taylor, who

had a sister called Ann, three years older than her. Ann used to worry about Jane because she was a rather delicate child. In fact, her father moved the family from London to Lavenham and then to Colchester to keep her well.

Jane developed into an imaginative child, who loved entertaining people. When they lived in Lavenham, they used to put her on the baker's kneading board, so she could be seen and heard telling her stories to a crowded shop, full of listeners. She was still rather a timid child, but Ann, with the help of the servants, kept an eye on Jane when she walked about the village muttering her verses.

The girls grew up in a house full of books. Their father, Isaac Taylor, did copper engravings for book illustration, and from early morning until dusk his five children helped him. They stopped only for meals, during which time the books were read aloud so the process of learning continued.

Ironically, when Isaac discovered that his children won poetry competitions, he said very emphatically that he did not wish his daughters to become authors, yet they did!

Amusingly, a London publisher read the children's poems when they appeared anonymously, and in 1804–05 he published *Original Poems for Infant Minds by several Young Minds*, including Ann, Jane and their brother Isaac.

Ann and Jane went on to write books for children which were well liked, especially the book with 'Twinkle, twinkle little star' in it. They may have been inspired by their father taking Jane to a series of lectures by an 'astronomer of repute' at the Moot Hall.

Moonlight had a special fascination for the family too. Jane would sit on a Roman wall reading poems to her friends by moonlight. When the family grew up and were separated, their father told them all to leave their houses at night for a few minutes and gaze up at the moon thinking of each other. And then, when Ann got married, Jane wrote on her own with her mother's encouragement, but sadly Jane died when she was 41. Ann lived longer but only occasionally wrote, about social issues like anti-slavery, prison reform and ethics. I must admit, it is Jane I admire, for she was a shy person who came to life through her imagination. That was what I was like as a child myself.

OLD KING COLE

They love festivals and feasting in Colchester, and so it seems appropriate that Old King Cole may have been a Colchester man. See what the nursery rhyme has to say about him.

Old King Cole was a merry old soul
And a merry old soul was he.
He called for his pipe
And he called for his bowl

And he called for his fiddlers three.
Every fiddler had a fiddle
And a very fine fiddle had he
Oh there's none so fair as can compare
With King Cole and his fiddlers three.

Like many nursery rhymes, no one knows who wrote the rhyme, but all the illustrations of him show a remarkably merry fellow who enjoyed music and food and his pipe, and the rhyme appears to have been composed about 1706.

So who was he? Finding a few clues, he seems to have been inspired by a Celtic king who gave his name to Colchester (Col was the first part of the king's name and Chester was the name for a fort, so putting the two phrases together made it 'Col's Fort', and this developed into 'Colchester').

Another clue might have been that he was the father of St Helena, and she was famous for going all the way to Jerusalem to find the

True Cross which grew as a tree at Golgotha, and relics of the Three Wise Men. Later on, Colchester put symbols of this journey on its town's shield, and the shield still has the same design. There was a cross on a green budding piece of wood against a blood red background, and three nails to remember the crucifixion of Jesus, and three crowns for the Three Wise Men.

Stand in front of Colchester Town Hall and look up to the very top. You will see a statue of St Helena carrying the cross, and inside the building there is a stained-glass window design of her. As for King Cole, he seems to be a very popular illustration in books of fairy tales and a good verse to chant. It's just a little strange that he always appears in a costume that seems more Tudor than Roman. Perhaps his story was much later in history. Maybe you will have ideas of your own about his story.

HUMPTY DUMPTY

Humpty Dumpty always provokes lively discussion as to what his historical origins might be. Again, we have no idea whose rhyme this might be. His name makes us smile, and even more curious is the idea that he is egg-shaped.

The nursery rhyme version, however, actually is quite complicated, as people in Colchester like to think of him as a cannon! This is what the rhyme actually says:

Humpty Dumpty sat on a wall
Humpty Dumpty had a great fall.
All the king's horses and all the king's men
Couldn't put Humpty together again.

Many people believe the small, egg-shaped mortar cannon appears in the story of the siege of Colchester, when the Roundheads attacked the king's men in 1648 during the English Civil War. The king's men tried to

protect their city, and in particular they put a cannon on St Mary's Church, which was fired by no less a person than 'One Eyed Jack Thompson'.

After a month, the Royalist fort inside St Mary's was blown to pieces, and the cannon known as Humpty Dumpty was damaged. So now the Royalists were very close to surrender. They just could not move their cannon because it was too heavy. So after all, the king's men could do nothing more to save Humpty Dumpty, and they did have to surrender to Parliament.

The drawing of Humpty Dumpty in *Alice Through the Looking Glass* shows him in his egg shape talking nonsense to Alice. So maybe it is right that Humpty had no connection with a piece of history, but he makes a wonderful comic character, whom many illustrators love to draw.

OLD MOTHER HUBBARD

We do know who wrote *The Comic Adventures of Old Mother Hubbard and her Dog*. It was a lady called Sarah Catherine Martin, the wife of a naval officer. Her husband used to get annoyed with the time she took writing her comic verses, but actually children loved her rhymes and they were popular for years after 1805, when she first wrote Mother Hubbard. Here are some of the verses:

Old Mother Hubbard
Went to the cupboard,
To give the poor dog a bone;
When she came there
The cupboard was bare
And so the poor dog had none.

She went to the baker's
To buy him some bread
When she came back
The poor dog was dead.

She went to the undertaker's
To buy him a coffin;
When she came back
The dog was laughin'.

The dame made a curtesy,
The dog made a bow;
The dame said 'Your servant'.
The dog said 'Bow-wow'.

This wonderful dog
Was Dame Hubbard's delight
He could read, he could dance
He could sing, he could write;
She gave him rich dainties
Whenever he fed
And erected this monument
When he was dead.

By now, I am sure you have realised that most
nursery rhymes were thought of as nonsense
and made many people smile. Some might

have a reference to genuine history, but by now it has become so buried in the past that we can't make sense of it. Apparently there was a reference to the doggie as being Henry VIII, and the bone as being his divorce from Ann Boleyn which Cardinal Wolsey had failed to grant him. Now, that is too hard for us today, but the rhyme was popular because the rhythms work well when they are read out loud for small children, and also they make good illustrated stories.

WHERE TO FIND A DRAGON

Funny, isn't it, how many people love dragons? There are so many kinds of dragons too – like a coccodil, a worm, a thirsty dragon and a basilisk? You can find them hidden all over Essex. They are, of course, always frightening, but there will be a rescuer if you wait long enough, usually a knight in shining armour.

THE COCCODIL IN THE WATER

To find the coccodil of Essex, you have to go to the sleepy village of Wormingford and find its pretty little church. Inside the church, there is a stained-glass window, which shows a maiden running from a knight who seems to be trying to kill a creature that looks very like a crocodile. This is how the story started.

When the English King Richard the Lion Heart was on his way home after fighting in the Crusades in the Holy Land, he was given an egg by Saladin. In case you don't remember, Saladin was the man he fought against, although they had always respected each other.

'An egg! Whatever is this for?'

Saladin smiled. 'It is to keep you safe.'

'How?'

The king never got an answer. He just saw Saladin disappear into the desert on his camel, sending the sand of the desert flying high. The king shrugged his shoulders and just put the egg into his saddlebag, muttering, 'I will have to go to Germany on my way home. I know that is a dangerous place, so I will look after anything that keeps me safe very carefully.'

To protect himself, he disguised himself as a pilgrim in long robes, but it did no good for very shortly afterwards he was kidnapped by Otto, Duke of Austria, who kept him in prison and demanded a ransom for him from the people of England.

It was very boring, waiting for the ransom to come through, so the king played with the egg until he noticed a crack was beginning to show up and the tiny face of a reptile began to show. He worried what it could be and was very relieved when the ransom arrived promptly.

He set off for England, making sure the egg was back in the saddlebag, and as they rode along he tried to amuse the little creature with cooing noises, but to his horror, the creature was getting BIGGER and BIGGER! It was so big it had to crawl along by the king's side

There was nothing for it, once he'd crossed the Channel, other than to take it to the menagerie keeper at the Tower of London. Immediately the menagerie keeper knew what it was, and he called it a 'coccodil' in that funny medieval way of his. Today we would call it a 'crocodile'.

'Majesty,' the keeper said, 'this coccodil is a fearsome creature. It will grow until it be twenty cubits long with a crested head and teeth like a saw and teeth extending to this length …' He tried to stretch his arms out to show the monster's size, but they weren't long enough.

'How shall we take care of it? It will eat us all up.'

'Build a strong cage, keep it locked up and well fed.'

The keeper did as was expected of him, but within the year, the creature had grown so big that his tail banged against the bars and the cage was smashed to smithereens.

With an almighty crash, the creature fought his way out of the cage and on and on through Essex it went. It was delighted to be free of its bars and it went sliding down the Essex rivers, smashing and slithering through the mud, always making sure it travelled at night so nobody saw him. The only evidence left behind in the morning were the dead bodies of young men and women it had killed.

Swimming, crawling and ravaging its way through the river, the coccodil came

to a village called Withermundford (which was the old name for Wormingford) on the River Stour. Total panic broke out when the people saw those jaws opening and closing – revealing spiked teeth from which nothing could escape. Not even arrows could pierce that impenetrable skin and the arrows tinkled against the stones of the riverbank.

Then it all got worse! The coccodil started demanding little children to eat for its lunch. All the parents began to cry, and then the lord of the manor demanded they send for Sir George from Layer de la Haye. Good old Sir George! He came as fast as he could, and came straight down to the ford where the creature waited.

It made him nervous, so he only encouraged his horse to advance three paces at a time, while lifting his lance high. Then the coccodil jumped up at him, aiming for the knight's sturdy legs. The knight was wearing a suit of black armour and even the coccodil could not bite his way into that suit of metal, and the creature found himself sliding off the horse into the water, leaving a trail of bubbles behind. All the village folk came down to the river shouting with delight that he had been dealt with so effectively.

Even today the water of the mere gets agitated from time to time. Bubbles rise to the surface. There is a whistling in the reeds and strange water plants wave desperately. The wise nod their heads, and know it can only be the descendent of the coccodil. Just watch and see where the bubbles go!

THE DRAGON WHO LOVED BEER

Call her what you like – sometimes she is known as the She Dragon of Great Bentley after the village, or sometimes the Drawsword Serpent after the field where she made her home.

One thing was very clear: it is not a good idea to leave a dragon in a field where she is a danger to lambs, small dogs and nervous old ladies. Committee meeting after committee meeting was held to discuss what to do about her, but nobody could think of anything.

Luckily, the landlord of the Plough Inn discovered the She Dragon was very fond of beer and she would get through a barrel of beer a day, which made her very sleepy. The only problem was it was very expensive, so

the parish council had to think of something else for the village to get rid of her.

I am sure by now you will have realised that there was nothing for it but to do what was usually done in these cases, which was to hire a knight in shining armour, so they sent for Sir Barry Woodruff of Brightlingsea, and a fine young knight was he.

In fact, he did a splendid job of slaying the She Dragon. He stuck his sword right through her vast belly and carried her still speared on his sword down to the village green, so everybody could see her. Great Bentley Green is one of the biggest greens in England and so a vast crowd was able to collect there. Unfortunately, Sir Barry Woodruff stumbled through the crowd, and as he held her aloft a spot of lethal venom from her massive jaws fell on his foot, and that was the end of him.

And what of the dragon? Well, there were occasional sightings of her and an odd hiss, which suggested she was still about. No doubt still looking for her beer. So, a little advice for you if you live in Great Bentley. Leave a bottle of beer on your doorstep to keep her and her children away from you.

THE TERRIFYING BASILISK

Saffron Walden is a very attractive market town in North Essex, with fine historic houses and a beautiful church that go back to medieval times, and green fields that have provided a good living for farmers for centuries, but there was a time once when everything went fearfully wrong and the town was cursed by one of the most fearsome creatures of all – a basilisk.

Nobody could believe it. Fruit rotted on the trees, birds dropped dead from the sky. The rivers were poisoned and there was a monster who lived in the fields, whose breath was so foul that anything that got in its way fell down dead! It was such an unbelievable story that not everybody believed it.

So in the end a vast crowd of townspeople made their way to the hill outside the town where the Wise Woman sat, to ask her what she knew about it, because she had the reference book called *The World's Most Dangerous Dragons*, but she was not prepared to read from it until somebody from Saffron Walden, who had seen the creature for themselves, would explain what it looked like.

It was a very serious farmer with a bobbing head who managed to describe what he had seen. He stood up very straight and announced, 'It had the head and claws of a rooster.' He paused, waiting, expecting laughter, but there was none. Something in the tone of his voice made the people believe what he said. The farmer went on even more alarmingly, 'It had the forked tongue of a serpent which swung backwards and forwards like … like the Devil. He walked upright with a very strong tail to keep his balance.'

'And what colour was he?'

'Black and yellow with a white spot in the middle of his head.'

So far the Wise Woman had listened carefully, but now she obviously was leaning forward earnestly on her skinny elbows and demanding to know, 'What were his eyes like?'

The farmer looked down at his feet sheepishly and said nothing.

The Wise Woman rose to her full height and said, 'I knew it. If you had looked into his eyes, you would be dead by now.' She shook her scrawny neck and looked at the crowd as though they were complete idiots. Screaming at them all she said, 'Don't you realise it's a BASILISK? See what it says in my book.' She held the book up and it said in large letters: 'A BASILISK

IS THE MOST DANGEROUS OF CREATURES. LOOK INTO HIS EYES AND YOU WILL DIE.'

The crowd clung to each other in desperate fear at what she had said. As usual, the mayor came up with the usual cure. 'Send for a knight in shining armour,' he instructed. It was the only thing to do, although it took several days and many miles to reach a knight with any real experience.

In the meantime, some foolish people went to see the basilisk for themselves, and sure enough immediately fell down dead when they looked into his eyes.

When the knight arrived, he was taken aback by how dangerous the monster was. He went immediately to his room in the inn and prepared his armour and weapons, and then read the *Knights Handbook* to find out all he could about basilisks, and this is what he found:

THE DANGERS OF BASILISKS

Its breath burns everything in front of it.
It cannot be defeated by a sword or a spear
for the poison from the weapon will flow
up the arm of the person holding it and
be deadly.
A glance from its eyes is fatal.

POSSIBLE CURES

The herb rue is known to help.
The beast only closes its eyes when he
drinks water from a clear pool.

The knight spent many sleepless hours
worrying how he could help the people. He
tossed and turned and tossed and turned trying
desperately to think what to do. Then you
know how it is – in the middle of the night we
sometimes get the answer to our problem. He
said nothing when he woke, just went about
his plan. It was a village boy who first noticed
his progress to the field where the monster lay.

'He's here. The knight is here. Hurrah!'

'What is he wearing?'

'Well, whatever it is, it is something I can see myself in the reflection.'

'I think I know what it is. It's a suit of armour made out of crystal mirrors.'

'What is the point of that? I can't understand it, for he carries no sword and only a sprig of rue.'

Yet still the crowd trusted him and followed the knight carefully to the field. They stopped when he stopped, and like him closed their eyes. Silence fell, and the basilisk rose to its legs and stared at the knight, its baleful eyes glittering with malice. Then, with a great shriek, he suddenly saw himself reflected in the armour's crystal plates and even he was horrified at his own image, and fell motionless to the ground. There was no more movement. He was still in death. It was the strangest passing, for looking into his own terrifying eyes had caused his death and his last heartbeats faded away.

Yet all around him an almighty roar echoed on all sides, as the people rejoiced that they were safe from harm. Drums, tabors and fiddles began playing and the people began to dance, and some say the dancing still goes on when people remember their great escape.

In fact, there used to be a memorial to the knight in Saffron Walden Church, but it got destroyed in the civil war. How sad! Perhaps we should rebuild a memorial to him in these troubled times. Courage and cleverness should always be celebrated.

STRANGE NEWS OUT OF ESSEX

Edward never forgot the summer of 1669, for that was the year he was nine years old and the dragon came to Henman. What excitement! Nobody could quite believe it. Nothing like this had ever been heard of in that part of Essex. To think that a flying serpent had come to little Henman, Henman on the hill! Now there were some people who called it a dragon, and older generations called it a worm, but there was something not quite right about the story.

Edward felt that the story told by the fine gentleman in the blue velvet suit was the most convincing. After all, it had been he who had caught the first sign of the dragon. 'Oh people!' he said. 'I was so frightened. It just came at me out of nowhere and it attacked me and my horse and was so enormous, I felt we were both in danger of death. I gripped my mare so tightly that her eyes rolled in panic. In the field beyond, I saw a farmer and screamed to him to move his cattle, or surely the dragon would get him and his herd. The poor man shook like an aspen. He just did not hesitate. With his dog at his feet and his droving stick is his hand, he shooed them into the cowshed. I didn't stop to see if they got there safely. I just wanted to get here and tell you all what was happening.'

A few days later, another story of the dragon came from two men, Harry and Sam, known for spending a great time in the pub. Now they said they had seen the dragon sunning itself on the hill. It had stretched itself out to its fullest extent, so it was possible to see just how enormous he was, and truly he was gigantic. The men had been too nervous to get up close, despite the fact that they were armed with clubs and staves. The dragon had rolled over, as though he was challenging them.

'Tell us more,' the people demanded. 'What did he look like?'

Harry took over the story with much gesturing of his arms. 'Now, the creature was at least 8 to 10 foot long, and the smallest part of it was the size of a man's leg, and his eyes were so large, and I am sure it was not the old man's drawing! The eyes were so piercing and his teeth were so very white and sharp.'

Sam, meantime, was doing own funny little drawing of the dragon. Edward thought he was out of proportion, for his wings were stumpy and looked too weak to carry such an unwieldy body.

More and more people arrived, wanting to know how the old men had coped, and they said it had been very difficult. Sam had gone off to get his gun and Harry had just stood there staring at the dragon. What did the dragon itself do? It ambled off to the woods grunting and groaning to itself.

Edward was puzzled. He could not understand why grown-up people believed in such nonsense? It went on all summer with men setting out with muskets, guns and fowling pieces all intent on finding the fearsome creature. What was really odd was all the people who went off to see the dragon came back looking remarkably cheerful.

What was going on? There must be some truth in it when people like the church warden, the constable and the overseer of the poor all claimed to have seen the dragon.

Then, one day Edward bumped into his cousin Noah. Noah thought he knew everything, and taking Edward by the arm led him to the Winstanleys' outhouse, and said, 'I've got something to show you.'

Edward was a little nervous at walking into the disused building, and even more so when he saw in the gathering dusk something lying in the straw that looked like some misshapen monster. He tried to walk away but Noah pushed him closer to it. Then he saw it seemed to be some curious object made of canvas and wood.

'Go on, you are meant to put it on your head, you big baby. Let me show you,' and he put the contraption over his own head, and sure enough he looked just like the dragon in the field.

'Who made a thing like that?'

'Henry Winstanley of course. Don't you remember those wonderful dragon kites he made? Well, he made this, and his uncle spread the news in his magazine of a wonderful new dragon.'

'But so many people believed this nonsense, even serious-minded adults!'

'Well, even adults like a joke, you know, and it makes for a rattling good story. Don't spoil it. Keep it to yourself. After all, it will make the village famous.'

For a while it certainly did. Henman had an annual fair to sell models of the monster. Even today, the village website is proud to have a dragon fluttering across their page. I can promise you that if a dragon turned up in Henman today, he would get a warm welcome. They like a joke there.

ARE YOU AFRAID OF THE DARK?

This is a story I helped invent, inspired by an African story and a boy I knew in Essex. It is very popular in my storytelling sessions, because everybody has things which frighten them.

I don't know what you are afraid of, but we had a boy called Jack in Brightlingsea, who seemed to be afraid of everything. He was afraid of the dark, he was afraid of being on his own, and afraid of being with other children.

His mother used to get very annoyed with him, and one autumn afternoon she sent him off to the woods to pick blackberries. He wasn't very pleased, because he knew the ripest berries were in the darkest part of the woods and that was the last place he wanted to go to, but somehow he managed to push his way right into the centre of the wood where he could see the glistening berries high up above his head. He practically had to stand on tiptoe to reach them, and just as he squashed a couple of berries between his fingers he heard a creature shriek with pain in the undergrowth. Fortunately, a glimmer of light shone through the branches of an aged chestnut tree, and he saw immediately that the animal was twisted up in the thorns of a bramble bush.

It was a hare, and foolishly it was desperately trying to free itself from the thorns. Fortunately, Jack had a gentle soft voice that stopped the hare struggling, and he was able to very carefully undo the animal from the bramble's branches. The hare looked up at Jack with twinkling dark eyes and muttered, 'Thank you so much. Now I owe you a favour, so whenever you are in trouble in the dark, look up at the moon and think of me and I will help you.' Before Jack could thank him, the hare was bounding through the wood, sending the fallen leaves crackling behind him.

Jack's mother was absolutely delighted with his blackberries. 'What a fine pie this will make for us tomorrow!' But it was late, and before he knew it, Jack found he had

been sent to bed without a light. He found to his horror that, he was laying in his bed in complete darkness, and some horrible string-like substance was stretched across his face. Then, luckily, he remembered the hare and the moon, and there was sufficient light from the moonbeams to show him that it was after all only the strands of a spider's web stretched across his face. How silly he felt!

The next night he went up again to his dark bedroom, and as he lay in his bed, he heard a scratch, scratch, scratch sound moving around the room. Jack, knowing the house was very old, muttered to himself, 'That sounds like rats running around the room in hobnail boots!' Once again he remembered the hare and the moon and he got up his courage and walked over to the window and listened carefully, and then saw what was happening. The wind had got up and was blowing the branches of the trees outside against the glass of the windowpane, so they made a loud scratching noise. He tittered to himself and muttered to himself, 'Just the wind in the trees!'

Jack's family had gobbled up the blackberry pie with real pleasure and he really thought he might be given a light of his own. Not likely, for his room on the third night was still dark and he could still hear some boys from school shouting up at him under his window, so he threw a football down to them and to his surprise he was encouraged to join in the game, and so he ran out into the moonlight. Amazingly he was kicking well and scoring goals. The boys were delighted, and punching the air with glee still cheered him on!

The next day he found himself walking down to the village, feeling very brave. To his surprise he found all the village people standing at the bottom of the hill, screaming and pointing to a hideous yellow and purple monster at the top of the hill. 'You are not frightened of that, are you?' he said in amazement and started stomping up the hill to examine it more clearly. Surprisingly, as he got closer the monster was falling asleep on his nose and actually seemed to be getting smaller and smaller.

Jack was amazed. He just picked the creature up and took it down to show everybody. He laughed. 'Surely you cannot be frightened of this tiny creature? It's no bigger than a frog,' and he passed it around everybody.

One girl asked, 'What is its name?'

'It's called *What might be*.'

And you see that's how it is. If you get up close to that creature called *What might be*, then it will shrink and you won't be frightened of anything that might happen in the future any more!

WHITE LADIES

Whenever a lady ghost appears in a story she nearly always wears white, and sometimes she is only seen as a vaguely misty figure who floats in the grey air. In Essex, sometimes smugglers told these alarming ghost tales in order to put off the customs men from finding their hidden booty. Down by the sea, the misty landscape of Canvey Island has a very special atmosphere which encourages the idea of a haunting.

THE SMELL OF VIOLETS

Charles Dickens, the famous author, was fond of ghost stories, and I have always believed that he got his idea for Miss Havisham, the old lady who sat by her crumbling wedding cake in her wedding dress in his novel *Great Expectations*, from this story of a ghost on Canvey Island.

Poor Lucy was not very happy; she had been left to clean up the bar room of the inn known as the Lobster Pot yet again. She had to wash the floor, to keep the fire lit and to clear away the mutton chops from last night's supper. She had had been left to do this all by herself and she was furious! Slop, slop, slop she slapped her cloth against the beer-stained table. Her mop cap kept falling down over her eyes, and her sacking apron was getting more and more greasy. She started to sing a very rude song, when to her embarrassment she realised a pair of laughing blue eyes were staring at her from the settle in front of her. It was Billy the sailor, who had obviously fallen asleep on the settle the night before.

'What lovely creature wakes me? Some fairy queen perhaps?' he grinned.

'Don't be stupid!' she muttered, and went to flick her cloth at his face, but he grabbed her wrist and kissed her not once, not twice, but three times! She actually enjoyed those kisses and that was how the romance began between Billy and Lucy. Everyone warned her against the one in the 'tarry trousers'. The other serving wenches warned her how unfaithful sailors could be, and her mother was determined she should marry the local tailor. He at least was respectable and well paid.

Billy, however, was determined to marry his Lucy, and made her promise they would be married at St Catherine's Church in the spring. First he had to go to sea. To prove his respectability, he bought her a ring to wear about her neck on a scarlet ribbon, but they did not tell her parents about their engagement.

For the entire winter Billy was away, the tailor came calling to court her. He told her mother, 'She's not interested, Mrs Godfrey.' Lucy would run off to her room to avoid her mother's nagging, and that's where she kept her secret. There she worked on the lovely white lace dress that she was going to wear for her wedding.

Slowly the sun was appearing and violets were coming into bloom. Spring was arriving at last, and Billy would be home soon. Then all of a sudden, her world felt like it was falling apart. A newspaper was put on the bar describing a terrible storm in Nova Scotia, and Billy's name was listed among the dead. Lucy cried so loudly even her mother knew something was very wrong.

For the next month Lucy just faded away, not speaking to anyone. She grew so thin she pined away and was buried in St Catherine's Churchyard in the lovely wedding dress she had worked so hard to make. Every spring, many of the people of Canvey Island caught a glimpse of the figure in white lace floating down Bride's Walk. There is a strong smell of violets, and people know it's Lucy's ghost and bow their heads in respect.

THE SONG OF JACKY ROBINSON

This is an old folk song that sounds very like Lucy's story, only with a happier ending:

JACKY ROBINSON
The perils and dangers of the voyage are past
And the ship at Portsmouth has arrived at last
The sails all furled and the anchor cast
And the happiest of the crews is Jacky
    Robinson.

He met with a man and he says 'I say
Perhaps you know one Polly Grey.
She's somewhere hereabouts.' The man
    replied,
'I do not indeed,' to Jacky Robinson.

In a public house they both sat down
And talked of admirals of High Renown
And drunk as much grog as came to half a
    crown.
This here strange man and Jacky Robinson.

When Jacky called out the reckoning to pay
The landlady came in, in fine array.
'Well damn my eyes, why here is Polly Grey
Who'd have thought of meeting here,' says
   Jacky Robinson

Says the lady, say she, 'I've changed my state.'
'Why you don't mean,' says Jacky, 'that
   you've got a mate?'
'You know you promised,' says she, 'I could
   not wait
For no tidings could I gain of Jacky
   Robinson.'

'And someone, one day, came up and said
That somebody else had somewhere read
In some newspaper how you might be dead.'
'I've not been dead at all,' says Jacky
   Robinson.

'But to fret and stew about is all in vain
I'll ship out to Holland, France and Spain

No matter where I'll ne'er come here again.'
And he was off before you say Jacky
  Robinson.

THE COLD GIRL AT EAST MERSEA

One of my favourite places in Essex is
Mersea Island, because it is full of romantic
stories and there are wonderful walks down
by the shore and the ships, and the chance
for lovely feasts of shellfish. The most famous
writer on the island was Sabine Baring
Gould, the vicar of East Mersea Church for
ten years, but his large family was never very
happy there and he called it 'Ten Years in
the Mud'. His daughter explains why it was
never an attractive place to live in the 1870s:

It smelt! They would bring the droppings
from the London Streets by barge to act
as manure and if it wasn't the stink from
the horse muck, then it was the sprats.

What a foul odour! And then the fields were guarded by boys with rattles, horns and drums to scare away the birds. Such a noise! And as for the mosquitoes – they swarmed so thickly that it looked like the trees were smoking. Mama used to burn laurel leaves over red hot coals to keep them away.

Yet we were lucky. Many of the poor women and girls on the island had to pick winkles for the London Market. Poor souls; many had boards tied to their feet and gliding about on these, they stooped to collect the molluscs into a basket on the left hand. It was horrible to see them if they fell. Many of the children were so poor they wore cut down uniforms from the garrison in Colchester. I heard Papa say to one girl:

'Hannah! You have not much clothes on and the weather is cold.'

And her answer was 'Oh! I've got my frock on and then comes oi'.

Our faces got so cold from the east wind we put cold cream on our cheeks. The cold got so bad it meant lots of people died. We heard a farmer say he lost three wives, two cows and four pigs and said 'Wives! You only have to hold up your hand and whistle and a score of Applications will come after you. Wives is very cheap but pigs is costly and cows is ruinous.'

Now Papa was a good preacher. Sermons were only ten minutes long but farmers complained they were not long enough for a nap. Miss Biggs our governess played the organ in the church. It wheezed like an old man with asthma.

Father used to frighten people too. He knew so much about werewolves, ghouls and those dreadful Icelandic

sagas. The wind whistled all the time on the island and I heard him tell our visitors that it was the plaintive cry of doomed sailors unable to reach the shore to dry their clothes and warm their frozen limbs.

Funny how stories spread. Mama and a friend went swimming in the moonlight and people said they'd seen mermaids! But I think that was Mrs Baker, the funny old girl who ran the ferry to Brightlingsea with her husband. She used to give us shrimps and tea and tell us wonderful stories. She wore an old military jacket she got from a soldier in Colchester. Trouble was, she was fond of the drink and sometimes her husband would lock her out and pour cold water over her head to sober her up.

I think this was one of Mrs Baker's invented stories, the one we used to tell about the ghost at the Dog and Pheasant.

THE GHOST AT THE DOG AND PHEASANT

This was the story that Baring Gould had often heard. It was said to have happened in the days of the Siege of Colchester, during the Civil War in 1648.

It had rained and rained all that summer and the farmers of East Mersea were convinced that their harvest would be ruined. The affairs of king and Parliament were nothing to do with them. All they could do was to sit grumbling over their pints in the Dog and Pheasant, wondering how they would last the winter. Their tempers got no sweeter when the red-haired boy called Tom came hurtling through the pub door.

'What's the matter with you, urchin?' old Barnby demanded.

The boy went pale and hung onto the old man's sleeve. 'Masters, come quick, the soldiers be at the church and be smashing the windows.'

This got the whole pub banging the table and shouting. They knew which soldiers these would be. They could only be Parliament's men. They were doing it all over East Anglia, smashing windows and breaking down statues of saints. What was the sense of that? The men of East Mersea did not take kindly to London men interfering in this way in their affairs. They picked up whatever tools might make useful weapons and set off like a miniature army, but as they got nearer to the church they slowed down and peered cautiously through the window.

It was obvious the soldiers had gone. The place was silent, but there was plenty of evidence that windows were open to the sky, and a beautiful rood screen lay smashed on the floor. Then a whimper came from the vestry, and it was the poor snivelling vicar. They bought him out carefully, but he was still angry that Parliament's men could think they could worship God in the way they did, destroying everything in the way they did.

'Where have they gone?'

'They have gone to the little garrison where there are still a few of the king's men left. We know what they have come for, they are going to make sure the Royalists have no food left.' The men went back to the village to make sure everyone knew what was happening.

In the days that followed, the news that came from Colchester was heartbreaking. It was said that people were having to eat dogs and cats and candle ends. They even took the thatch off the roof to feed their horses. The tower of St Martins came tumbling down and the priory of St Botolph's was a bare skeleton. Apparently, all the parliamentary leader could say was, 'Let them eat horseflesh and maggots until disease gets them.'

Young Tom and the landlord's daughter, Ann, a spirited girl with flashing dark eyes and black hair, talked a lot about what could be done, until eventually her father could be seen taking bundles down to the cellar, but sadly somebody talked too much and there came a fierce knocking at the door. Dragoons! It was a band of parliamentary dragoons and their strict captain with his stiff beard.

'Open the door,' he demanded, and then he wanted the cellar opened up. The landlord tried to block the cellar by standing against the door.

'Come on you bumpkin, do as I say.'

No movement except for footsteps coming down the stairs. They turned to look. It was Ann, shouting, 'Leave my father alone,' but it did no good. The captain had raised his musket right into her face. He stared with horror as the smoke cleared and cursed his weapon for being so unreliable. Her father could not believe she was dead. They took her outside to revive her, but blood was seeping across her nightdress and her face was alabaster white.

It is said that even to this day her white form haunts the marshes, and her voice is heard whispering, 'Take care of my people.' And the wildfowl sing her praises and call for her protection.

TWO HUSBANDS, THREE GHOSTS AND ME

People always want to know where I get my stories; the most unusual way I heard of a story was through three people who had heard it from ghosts who lived in their various houses. It was not frightening but it was an unusual story, for it was about a beautiful lady who had two husbands! You don't believe me? This is how it happened.

It was a hot day in Brightlingsea in 1742, and the customs officers had come down to investigate a ship that was coming up the Colne very, very slowly. It had attracted their attention because it was piled high with boxes. They stopped the ship and questioned the young man in the prow about what was in them and where he had come from. He did not seem eager to talk. He looked very forlorn, pale and was wrapped in a velvet cloak. He gave his name as Mr Williams from Vienna, and explained that he had been on his way to Harwich when a strong storm had come up and he found he was on his way to Colchester.

The chief customs officer, John Todds, was not satisfied with this answer. He needed to know more. 'What is this about?' he asked and he pointed at his officers, who were busy searching through the boxes on the deck. Out had tumbled fine dresses, petticoats, corsets and ribbons, jewels and furs.

The young man shrugged his shoulders as though it were nothing to do with him, and then suddenly stared at one of the customs officers, who had suddenly drawn his cutlass and plunged it through the largest box of all, which was of plain deal. Mr Williams's face turned white and he shook with horror.

'No, don't do that,' he screamed, and the terror in his voice made everyone stand still, and then the lid of the box fell open and everyone saw what it was. It was a fine coffin with a large silver plate and the embalmed body of a beautiful young woman. The young man knelt by the coffin and he shook with tears. At last John Todds had sympathy for him. He patted the weeping young man's shoulder sympathetically. 'Who is this?'

'It is the body of my wife.'

'Your wife!'

Mr Williams sighed deeply. 'I am taking her to be buried at Thorpe-le-Soken,' and that was all he managed to say.

John Todds looked at him suspiciously. He was beginning to wonder. It was the custom in those days for a body to be buried in the land where the person died. This was all very suspicious. Transferring a body across the sea was just not done. Did he have a murderer on his hands? Best thing to do was to lock him and the body up for the night at the Church of St Leonards on the Hythe. Far more investigation was needed. It was too late to do anything else now.

The next morning, it seemed the young man had not moved all night except to cling on to his dead wife's hand. His story had spread around the neighbourhood and people came in and out to see if they could find out any more. An elderly couple from Thorpe-le-Soken seemed to be the most curious of all. The husband turned to look at his wife, and holding hands the couple stepped up to stare at the dead girl. A gasp came from the husband. 'Why! That's our vicar's wife!' he said.

The young man looked horrified but at last admitted to the truth. 'I see I must tell the truth after all. I am no Mr Williams from Vienna. I am in fact Lord Dalmany, son of the Earl of Roseberry, and I married this beautiful girl and we went on a romantic tour

of Europe. Then when we reached Verona …'
With this his eyes filled with tears … 'my
dearest Kitty became very sick and at last
admitted she had had a husband before me:
no less a person than Alexander Gough, vicar
of Thorpe-le-Soken. "It is a dreadful thing,"
she said, "to be a bigamist. If I should die, take
me back to be buried in Thorpe-le-Soken, as
it would be more appropriate."'

No one knew what to make of this. It was
thought that night that it was safe to lay the
dead lady in the Church of St Leonards on
the Hythe with the young man by her side.

The elderly couple squeezed the young
man's arm comfortingly, and the wife said,
'We remember her well. A pretty little
thing, and came from a background of solid
farmers. Dashing young men from Mistly
and St Osyth came a-courting her, but she
chose the vicar. She thought he'd make her
a respectable husband, but you know what
girls are? Respectability is boring! She got

fed up with him and his dusty books, so she goes up to London and goes to parties where she must have met and married you. So in the end it was not just one man, but two men that she deceived. What a girl!'

The story was so amazing that it spread rapidly, and no less a person than the vicar of Thorpe-le-Soken turned up himself, carrying a sword, ready to plunge it into the young man, but when he saw the tears in the young man's eyes he felt sorry for him. And so it was that both men walked up the aisle of Thorpe-le-Soken Church (arm in arm) to the flagstone under which Kitty was buried.

Neither of the men married again. Lord Dalmany died two years later at the age of 31, and the vicar survived for another twenty-two years. So where did the ghosts come into the story? Well, first of all I met a lady who lived in a cottage in Thorpe-le-Soken where the vicar had lived.

The second ghost was Kitty herself, who appears at a pub called The Bell at Thorpe. Apparently she moves the furniture about there and her portrait survived a fire in 1999.

And the third ghost … Well, guess who he was and where he lived? It was the ghost of customs officer John Todds, who lived in the same Brightlingsea house as I did from 1986 to 2017. I never actually saw him, but when I lifted the mat in front of the Lady Chapel in All Saints Church in Brightlingsea, I read this rhyme on his grave:

Farewell vain world, I've known enough
   of thee
And now am careless what thou sai'st of
   me.
Thy smiles I court not, Nor thy friends
   I fear:
My race is run, my head lies quiet here:
What fault you saw in me, take care to
   shun.

And look at home there's enough there
   to be done.

There are plenty of strange things to see in Brightlingsea graveyard, including the tomb of John Selleto, who always said he did not believe in God and said he would only believe in Him if an ash tree grew from his grave, and sure enough it did, and grew so big it had to be uprooted 170 years later and the tomb rebuilt.

INVADERS

Along the coast of Essex are 90 miles of indented waterways which over the centuries many people have come to invade – the Romans came and settled for some time, followed by the Saxons, then continual raids by the Vikings and then the Normans spread their power.

THE GHOST OF THE ROMAN CENTURION

Roman remains are dotted all over the county, but I have always been fascinated by the Mersea Barrow. It's not easy to find, as the barrow has shrunk from its original height and the modern road to the village of East Mersea is so close to its base it's not easy to see when you are driving along. It just seems like a hillock underneath an unkempt grove of trees.

There is nothing to suggest the excitement of May 1912, when a central shaft was dug through the mound by the archaeologist

Hazzledine Warren, who found a beautiful glass urn containing cremated remains wedged tightly in a lead casket. It seemed a strange thing, for the cremated remains were a Roman method of burial but the barrow itself was a way of respecting the death of a Celtic person of importance. Hazzledine Warren came to the curious conclusion that there was a ghost there, but a 'ghost not possessing any notable or distinctive personality'.

It's interesting to note that in 1912 the burial urn in its lead casket was removed from the tomb, and transported to Colchester Castle in a ramshackle car. Much to everybody's delight, it was recently brought back safely to the museum at Mersea, where you can see it now.

The story told most often, however, is the story of the ghost of the Roman centurion, and there are even modern-day sightings of this ghost. The most popular version is the

one told by Mrs Jane Pullen, the landlady of
the Peldon Rose.

She said:

He came off the Barrow Hills. The
steady tramp of a man's feet like a soldier
marching and he caught up with me all
the way down to the Strood.

I could see no one, yet the feet were
close behind me, as near as I could have
touched him. I bopped down to look
along the road in the moonlight. Still the
feet kept on. I walked along the road till
I came to a man I knew. He was all of a
tremble. He shook like a leaf.

'I can hear him,' he said. 'But where is
he? I can't see anyone.'

'Keep along with me,' I said to the man,
'and no harm will come to you. 'Tis only
one of the old Romans come out of the
barrow to take his walk. Besides, these
Romans will do you no harm. Put your

trust in God. And when you do that naught can harm you. Those old Romans can do you no harm.'

Now, my storytelling friend Andy Jennings saw the picture more clearly in his mind, for the Essex Storytellers had decided that the true story was about a Celtic chief who fell in love with a Roman maiden and sadly she had died. The chieftain had buried her cremated remains in the mound, according to the rites of his people. But then sadly a Roman centurion, who as a young man had also dearly loved her, came back to Mersea, after being away fighting many battles, with the intention to claim her for his own, only to find she was dead!

Imagine, as he gets nearer to the island, he hears the sound of mourners chanting the songs of the dead. The rain beating down on his face confuses him. He can see water on either side of him and realises that he has reached the Strood, the causeway linking Colchester to Mersea.

He is tired and dismounts from his horse, and looks back at the place of battle and see ghostly faces of the men who have fought with him, who whisper, 'Do not return to the island. Only grief awaits you there.'

He cannot stop himself. He must return to his home. A thick fog surrounds him and he cannot see the tide rising over the causeway, and he feels only the cold, and finds he is ankle deep in water and the distance to land is too great. He awaits his doom. The pull of the water is too great. He slips, numb to everything but his own pain and loss. He sinks, dragged by his own armour, 'a heart that died before it stopped beating'. And so his ghost still comes to remind us of the power of love.

THE HEROES OF THE BATTLE OF MALDON

After the Romans left, the Anglo-Saxons came into Essex, followed by the Vikings on their terrifying raids, bent only on plunder and theft. The story that people remember best is the poem of the Battle of Maldon which was written by an Anglo-Saxon poet in 991. The leader of the Anglo-Saxons at the battle was Byrhtnoth, ealdorman of Essex. He has two memorials to him, the statue in the alcove at the side of All Saints Church and a more modern statue at the end of the prom. In 2000 we Essex Storytellers had the honour of reciting a modern version of the poem. I am going to tell the story in prose, sometimes lapsing into the strong poetic rhythms of that time.

It all began when Byrhtnoth, a fine tall man, nearly six foot nine with long flowing silver hair, waited with his army on the River Blackwater and watched as ninety-three Viking ships sailed to Northey Island. They had come to demand gold and silver, but the Saxon thanes would give them none, although many wished they would. The women would be glad to save the inevitable deaths, the children were terrified of being taken as slaves, the old men heard what happened at Ipswich – fire, plunder, death and devastation – and wanted none of it. Wise men knew that to give in to the sea wolves' demands would mean they would come again, and Byrhtnoth made it clear that he would fight to the last against the heathens.

The battle begins when the tide changes, then Byrhtnoth allows the Vikings to leave the island and both sides had crossed the causeway, fighting on open ground. The heathen charge the Anglo-Saxon wall of shields. Spears and bows fly into a fierce wave of falling warriors, some wounded, some dead.

Despite his age, Byrhtnoth had fought off two of the Vikings, when he was hit by a spear and a Viking axe hacked into his shoulder.

Even in his dying moments, he cries 'I'll conquer yet' and he raises his massive sword with its gold hilt high, and prays for God to take his soul and for the Devil to come nowhere near him.

Sadly, Godric, one of his own men, betrayed him by riding away on Byrhtnoth's horse with his two brothers into the safety of the woods. The rest of the Saxon army remembered what Byrhtnoth had said to them, 'Always advance, never retreat,' and

that's what they did, despite the fact that so
many died. So it was written in the way of the
poet who recited it to drumbeats:

> Shield rims snap and chain mail sings,
> Sings a fearsome, gruesome Hymn
> The dead are many, the seamen surge,
> Wives of the dead men sing their Dirge
> Byrhtnoth, Byrhtnoth, Byrhtnoth,
> Byrhtnoth, Byrhtnoth!
> Troops of the Household shout.

> On and on the battle raged
> Until the dying of the light,
> The hunters of booty, the widows and
>   orphans
> Came to search among the dead
> But in the darkness they can see little.
> The mud and the maiming
> Have so mangled men
> That only a strip of embroidery or a cloak
>   clasp

Proves who lies among the swirling
    seagulls.

Maldon's battle is done!
The Saxon fyrd, once mighty
Lies broken.
Wounds savage and deep scar many a face
    and body.
Cold white bodies lie stripped
Of armour and weapons. Limbs severed
    and maimed
Greet the eyes of those who search.

Lifted from the field of his last battle
Byrhtnoth the ealdorman of Essex
The trusted one of King Ethelred
The grand old man
The tallest of men is taken home.

Shall his men be forgotten?
The names of the dead are recited
Memories fail and fade.

NO!
We will make a great Tapestry of what we
   have witnessed
All winter long shall our needles fly
Drawing in silk what we saw.
The glittering sword of Byrhtnoth as he
   fell in his last agony.
The traitor flying on his mighty bay
The shield wall broken
The tide's rise and fall
In this desolate place.

Then somewhere a harp is played
   At last the poet finds his voice
And the names he sings
Are taken on the wind
And as time passes
This epic tale of the men of Essex's
   unfailing courage
Shall pass from mouth to mouth
From one millennium to another
Curlews call.

The water laps
And the tale is retold.

THE VIKING WHO LOST HIS SHIPS

I love telling stories based on fragments of history and it means I have to do a lot of research, so I have to travel all over Essex, meet all sorts of knowledgeable people and explore the dusty shelves of local history libraries, and I thoroughly enjoy it all. One character I encountered in my wanderings was a man called Wentworth Day, who is dead now but whose books tell us so much about the past. He was actually a journalist, but he found most of his information while he was out hunting, shooting and fishing. Many of the characters he met were often very rough but they had grand tales to tell.

When I was looking for information about the Vikings, I came upon Wentworth

Day talking to a man called Charles Stamp, living in a shanty cottage facing the Thames under the sea wall at Canvey Island. Like many sailors he knew a great deal about the history of seafarers and was very superstitious. He was fascinated by the tall, blond man who haunted his house. He told his story in a broad Essex dialect, which I hope you try to understand because he makes everything come to life so vividly. Do read it aloud. Here is his tale:

I laid in my truckle bed upstairs one night last week and I looked over the top of the wall and saw the tide aflowing in. Bright moonlight that was. Bright as day. All of a sudden I seed a man come wading ashore. He was knee deep when I fust clapped eyes on him, kickin' up the spray. He got into the mud and came straight to this cottage. He knew how to walk on mud too, long striding strides same as you and

I when you don't dig your toe and heels. Otherwise you'd get stuck. Well he sort of skated across the mud, same as us, got into the saltings, jumped a rill or two and then came over the top of the sea wall. He crossed the plank over the dyke and next thing I knowed he was in my room. Tall handsome chap he was with long golden hair flowing down like a gal's. He wore a sort of tunic with a leather jerkin over it and cross gartering below his knees. He had a long droopy moustache, a rare old snout on him like an eagle, blue eyes and a helm on his head. That must have been steel cos it flashed in the moonlight. And there was a pair of wings sticking out of it, one on each side. He looked downright sorrowful and said, 'Mate, I lost me ship. I want to git home beyond the seas. Can you help me?'

'Go you down to Grays or Tilbury, owd mate,' I says. 'There's forever o' the ships come in there. You find one to take you to any port in the world.'

He looks at me again, shook his head and said sorrowfully like, 'You don't understand. I've lost me ship. I've lost my country. I'm a lost man.'

And with that, sir, he went out of the winder, all six foot of him, and over the sea wall, across the saltings and down under the mud and into the tide. He waded under the moon, his helm flashing in the moonlight, and then he vanished. The sea swallered him up. Who do reckon that was, sir?

Well, I am sure some of you have guessed this ghostly visitor was a Viking, but a rather old-fashioned picture of one, since history books don't show Vikings now with helmets with wings. Now, the problem is, do we know if it was a special Viking? A good guess would be the Viking leader Haesten the Black. The first mention of him was spending winters with his warriors on Mersea Island, then he moved south to Benfleet.

Benfleet was just the place for him, because it had water and timber in abundance and was hidden from the main stream. So there they could build their ships, and it was well suited to be a fortified camp. Haesten took advantage of this and went plundering in the surrounding area in order to get supplies. He left eighty ships behind him, thinking he had left enough men to guard his wife and children and other wives and children.

He was to have a shock, for behind a thick forest and marshland an Anglo-Saxon army was emerging, led by King Alfred's son Edward and his son-in-law Ethelred, who had come up from London. Nobody was prepared for this attack. What a shock! Viking ships were burnt down to the waterline or taken to London. Men were killed. Some ran away to Shoeburyness.

An even bigger shock for Haesten was that his wife and children were taken prisoner. Luckily, he found Alfred owed him a favour, for he was the children's godfather. It had happened after an early skirmish. Alfred, being a good Christian, returned the Viking's family when Haesten returned.

Mind you, the fighting continued for a while. Haesten, however, seems to have vanished despite his reputation as a 'lusty and terrifying old warrior'. Maybe he wandered around looking for his ships. Maybe he hesitated about attacking Arthur after his children were returned to him. He may have returned to sea, or maybe not!

It's a shame his ghost could not have returned in 1855, for he would have caught a glimpse of his old ships, for in that year navvies working on a local railway line did actually find the burnt-out timber of old ships.

OLAF OF THE SHORT FAT HAIRY LEGS
A MIGHTY SAGA OF THE NORSE FOLK

Part of the problem of trying to retell Viking and Saxon stories to modern audiences is that they find them very savage. I once tried to tell the story of the monster Grendal and his mother from the epic *Beowulf* to a class, but the children found it too alarming, so to cheer them I told them the tale of Olaf of the Short Fat Hairy Legs, which I have to admit was really something I made up myself to sound like a Viking saga.

Listen, and I will tell you the saga of Olaf of the Short Fat Hairy Legs.

Now, it all began on a morning when Olaf overslept. Panic-stricken, he raced to Benfield beach. Oh no! He could see the warriors' hordes in their long boats sailing away far out in the whales' way.

Then he realised his luck! 'How wonderful! Oh bliss! No more pillaging and plundering for me today! Today I can play with the seals,' but when he got to the next beach there were no seals. It was too cold for them.

Olaf sat on a rock and sulked, and then he began to realise his tummy was rumbling. He had had no breakfast! He reached in his pouch and found some of yesterday's cartwheel cake there!

As he tossed a handful of crumbs to his mouth, he felt something nudge him.

'You're hungry too,' he said, putting a generous slice of cake into the hand that had appeared at his side, but then he looked again. It was not a hand at all! It was a claw, and a claw that was going up and up into the mouth of a mighty monster. He was sitting on the knee of a monster who was nearly eighteen foot tall!

He had to really tilt his head backwards to see her properly. Oh my dears, what a hideous sea monster looked down at him. Every inch of skin was covered in green and purple bumpy warts. She had bulging eyes and great folds of flesh stretched across her belly. Olaf could not control himself. He started to shake with fear.

Then, to his total astonishment, she gave him a cuddle! It had been a long time since anybody had cuddled him and it made him want to cry.

'Please don't cry. Tell me, what troubles you?'

Olaf found himself telling her his most important secret. Something he had never said out loud to anyone. 'I am a failure. I will never make a proper Viking! I am no good at being brave and fierce.'

'There, there, don't take on so. I shall make you a great hero, fit to sit in the halls of Valhalla.'

'Me! A hero! Really?'

'Just remove my tail.'

He looked puzzled.

'Remove my tail!' she repeated.

'But won't it hurt you?'

The monster tut-tutted. 'Don't you know anything? We reptiles are always losing our tails and they always grow back again.'

This made Olaf feel a little happier, but he stared hard at her six-foot-long tail! It would take hours to cut through that with his axe.

The sea monster was getting very impatient. 'Pull it, you fool,' she shouted.

'Well, I'll try.'

It was not easy to get a good hold on her slimy skin, but to his amazement when he dug his heels into the sand and tugged with all his might, the tail came away with ease! He fell over backwards, still nursing the tail to his chest.

The sea monster laughed a funny, gurgling laugh. 'Now you have a trophy to take to the Great Hall. Go and bring back your fellow warriors, and I will stage a splendid death scene for them. Death scenes are my speciality. Many a Viking has tipped me a barrel of pickled herring for my trouble.'

It was not easy pulling the great tail up the beach. Olaf plodded manfully up the shingle and along the sand dunes, lugging his prize until he felt as though his arms would come out of their sockets. Every time he took two steps forward, he slipped back one in the heavy sand!

It took him a long time, so it was dark when he at last reached the Great Hall. From the din coming from inside, he knew that the warriors were back and that they were drunk. Olaf sighed and flung open the great door, but nobody turned to look at him.

Olaf could stand it no more, and bought down his hand so hard on the table that all the goblets danced in the air. 'Listen to me,' he bellowed.

Silence fell, and eighty pairs of bloodshot eyes turned to look at him.

Olaf felt very awkward. Somehow, he managed to speak. 'I, Olaf of the Short Fat Hairy Legs, have wounded the great sea

monster herself. I bring her tail to hang among the trophies of this great hall.'

Then came the shouts.

'You did it?'

'Olaf of the Short Fat Hairy Legs!'

'Why, he can't even slice the top off an egg!'

Curious, the great chief himself, Rig-of-the-Droopy-Drawers, came down from his throne to examine the tail and announced the truth.

Now the chief had spoken, cheers broke out.

'He's done it!'

'Good old Olaf!'

'But where is the body?'

The hall became full of shouts of, 'Where is the body?'

'She's on the beach.'

'The beach! Let us go to the beach!' came the shouts. With one accord the drunken mob rose to their feet and surged out into the darkness. Warriors stumbled over giggling girls, women fell over their crying children and children slithered and slid. The torch bearers were in such a hurry that sparks flying from their torches nearly set alight the maidens' hair.

It was worse for Olaf. With his short fat hairy legs, he could barely keep up. He got pushed to the back and reached out to steady himself, and found to his delight that he was holding the hand of the beautiful plump maiden with the fine plaits whom he had fancied for some time.

'Did you really do it?'

'Yes!' he said firmly, although usually he was very bad at telling lies.

Then the torch bearers were shouting, 'The monster is here!'

Out of the darkness the sea monster rose on her hind legs, and with a hiss of choking smoke from her great jaws she stretched out her horny claws above the heads of the crowd, so they fell back in horror.

Olaf emerged from the back, shouting, 'Leave her to me,' but he was confused as to what he should do.

'Grab that branch, you fool,' the sea monster hissed at him and then she moved in such a way that it looked as though every time he touched her with the branch, Olaf had inflicted a terrible blow.

She moaned. She groaned. The sand flew. They bobbed and circled each other menacingly, and then the branch was pointing at her great belly. She doubled over in mock agony, and fell to the ground so heavily that it felt as if the earth itself was being released from the hold of the Midgard Serpent and would crack apart.

The sea monster lifted her head one final time and gave a piteous cry that seemed to still the very motion of the waves.

Many of the warriors had become so frightened that they had run back to the Great Hall.

Only the maiden with the fine plaits moved closer to the sea monster, and leant over and rubbed her neck soothingly. She commanded full funeral honours. Drums beat. Horns were blown. The body was put on a ship drawn by blubbery white creatures, bedecked in shells, who guided the ship to the frozen oceans.

Then Olaf knew the full glories of being a hero, but the greatest wonder of all was that the girl with the fine plaits consented to be his bride.

Time passed and time passed. Olaf and his wife had five children – four boys and one girl. The girl was the youngest, and a troublesome thing this was for her too. When the boys wanted to play their favourite game, 'the day Father killed the sea monster', guess who had to play the part of the sea monster? The girl of course!

She got so tired of this that one day she ran into the house to her mother.

Her mother patted her comfortingly. 'I'll tell you a secret. Your father never really …'

She was just about to say 'your father never really killed the sea monster', when they felt a shadow from the doorway. It was Olaf himself. 'Do you mean to tell me that after all these years you knew I never really killed the sea monster?' he said.

His wife nodded and said how that was how it was.

'And you went on loving me?'

She nodded again.

Olaf smiled at last. Someone had loved him, just as he was! This was a secret worth having!

Ruffians and Rascals

We all have a secret liking for ruffians and rascals, and it's always been true that the best-known stories in Essex have always been about those wicked men with twinkling eyes – pirates, smugglers and highwaymen. I knew there was a story about an oak that grew from a pirate's heart, and I decided that the most beautiful oak tree I had seen was the one that grew by the duck pond in the pretty village of Fingringhoe, and it must have been the centre of the story, so this is what must have happened:

PIRATE JAKE AT FINGRINGHOE

Peg Leg Jake, that wild pirate from Doneyland, was coming home from sea after a long voyage, and he was so delighted! Now, you would have thought he would have gone first to see his mother in her cottage at Rowhedge, but that day something else was on his mind – his lovely girlfriend Rosie.

He was going up the hill to the Whalebone Inn at Fingringhoe to see her, for that was where she worked as a barmaid. It was a steep hill up to the inn. Thump, thump he went on his new wooden leg, feeling a little more cheerful for he had plenty of golden pieces of eight in his pocket and no dratted parrot weighing down his left shoulder. The foolish bird had fallen dead off his perch only yesterday, so his splendid new jacket was free of bird droppings and he had such tales of swashbuckling and adventure to tell her. Must be worth a kiss or two!

He could barely contain his excitement as the door of the inn swung open and there she stood, pretty as a picture in her frilly cap and apron. He put his hand up to lift her chin, to put a real smacker of a kiss on those ruby lips, but she swiftly moved her head out of his way and gave him a noisy slap on the cheek, and moved over to the table to pick up a full tray of foaming tankards.

'Leave me alone, I am busy,' she snapped, and out she went to the garden with the tray. He longed to follow her and her heavy burden out there, but he could hear the hearty sound of men's voices singing and knew what was going on.

Hearts of oak are our ships,
Jolly tars are our men
We always are ready,
Steady, boys, steady
To victory we call you again and again.

So that was it! Members of His Majesty's navy were in the village, and all the village girls had eyes for nobody else but the young sailors in their dashing uniforms. Even Rosie was bewitched by their tales of daring and their pockets clanking with money.

Jake turned back into a gloomy corner of the bar and nursed a small mug of beer, but then he got braver and he ordered a whole bottle of rum. Of course, this made him more and more depressed, and drunker and drunker. Even the landlord felt sorry for him. 'Come on old fellow, home with you. You know how it is, the navy must be served first. Tomorrow they'll be gone and you'll have Rosie all to yourself.'

Grunting, Jake got to his feet unsteadily and two sturdy sailors got him to the door. He was grateful, but still demanding to see Rosie. A great belch came out of his mouth and the men pushed him out of the door. 'She won't want to see you like this!'

They were right, of course. With a great effort he tried desperately to walk around Pig Foot Green without stumbling, until he fell over a bucket. It was the pigs' swill bucket and Jake found many acorns rolling under his feet. He picked one up gingerly and called out to the night sky. 'Hearts of oak, that's what we need.'

The noise woke an old woman sleeping in her bed in the cottage on his left-hand side.

'Shut your mouth, you silly fool,' she cried, and to make sure that he obeyed her, she reached out of her window and poked her broom into his back. An acorn went flying in the air and landed in his open mouth. He staggered forward and found he was close to the village duck pond. He felt as though his heart was cracking, and he found the pain sent him flying down on his back.

It was not until the next day that they found him lying there dead by the pond, and the vicar had to be sent for, so a funeral could be arranged. Poor Rosie was beside herself with grief, and when the villagers tried to comfort her, she managed to blurt out, 'He had a fine heart.'

They did not bury him in the church because he was a pirate. He was just left on the green with meadowsweet and wildflowers growing over him, and they never told the girl about the oak sapling that grew from his body, but today many people stop to gaze at that

wonderful old oak and remember the pirate's heart. There was something warm about him.

Hard Apple Will Smuggles at Paglesham

Now, all those pretty villages, especially on the eastern Essex coast, with their taverns full of tunnels hiding hidden booty, very quickly built up a romantic reputation, and many are their secrets of cunning smugglers.

In the isolated village of Paglesham, in the old days, if you ever walked into the village shop in daylight you would have met someone who seemed such a respectable village shopkeeper and church warden called William Hard Apple Blight. Yet, if you looked for William at night, then things were very different. You would find him out on the river bringing in rum, brandy and silk smuggled from France in his own cutter called the *Big Jane*.

Paglesham was, of course, a place where the smuggling trade did well. It was said there was so much smuggled gin in the village that it was used to clean the windows! And old William himself was fond of his booze.

On one occasion when he got captured by the customs men, he shouted to them, 'Have a drink with us,' and so they did, not just one drink, not just two drinks, but many more, so the customs men got so drunk that they had no idea that the smugglers' stolen goods had been slipped back again to the smugglers' own cutter, and not only that, but they captured other casks the revenue men had confiscated from other smuggler gangs! All done under cover of the drunken shouting and singing, so the smugglers were better off than when they started!

Sometimes, on other occasions, it got a little harder, for once William to his horror found himself tied hand and foot and thrown into the hold of the revenue men's ship, when

the ship ran aground on the Goodwin Sands.
Nothing for the revenue men to do but to
get the smugglers to move the revenue boat
off the sands and on its way, and so after all
William proved his cunning and got all those
men of the sea home safely and won them
their freedom.

That old rascal lived to be 74 years old and
was buried in Paglesham Church graveyard!
No wonder William was called the king of
smugglers. He was so brave and certainly
knew the ways of the ocean.

THE DARK HOUSE OF ROWHEDGE

Rowhedge in smuggling times must have
been the village with the biggest collection
of rascals, and even today the villagers there
are proud of the smuggling families that have
lived there for generations. When I went to
tell stories in their village hall, the people told

me all about the ruffians in their families. In fact, nearly every pub has a story to tell.

In a splendid red-brick pub, The Darkhouse, with its porch of white pillars, lived pretty Miss Molly with her golden hair and blue eyes, and her fancy man was no less than Captain John Pim. He would know if it was safe to come up the river with his illegal cargo if Molly had set up her signal. The signal was a lifted blind in the front window, and a lit candle where her much-petted fat black cat called the Bosun sat and kept an eye on the world. Then, when all the contraband had been given out to various hiding places in the village, the captain would kiss his sweetheart goodbye and go on to the Hythe at Colchester to sell all his legal cargoes. Now, amazingly the pair did eventually marry, and the captain moved into the 'Dark House', still doing a little smuggling on the side.

THE LADY SMUGGLER OF LEIGH-ON-SEA

Leigh-on-Sea is one of the most handsome and quaint of coastal towns, and there lived a lady called Elizabeth Little, and such a dainty lady she was! She was known to entertain with fine dinners with good food, splendid wine and educated conversation. She sold fine silk, lace, perfume and gin of the best quality. Few at her table knew she had a secret underground room with direct access to the waterside, which made smuggling an easy trade, and her family of brothers did the hard work on the boats while she had the organising skill.

On one occasion, this got her out of serious trouble. She and her family had managed to escape the coastguards on their way home on the Thames near Shoeburyness. It was a near-run thing. The coastguards shot at them and one of the brothers was wounded.

'Nothing for it,' said she, 'but to make for Barling Creek. They can't follow us there.

Now,' she said to her elder brother, 'you will take the empty boat right under the coastguards' noses. The rest of us will make our way overland.'

'But how will we do that?'

'Word has been sent to the undertaker from Little Wakering, and he is bringing us a coffin and hearse. Our wounded brother will hide in the coffin and all the contraband will go in the hearse, and see what a little handsome widow I will make with this black shawl over my head,' she tittered.

So the funeral procession set off, and actually got as far as Leigh Hill when they had a bad moment. A customs officer was standing by the side of the road. Luckily, in those days people were very respectful when a funeral went past. The officer tipped his hat and cast his eyes to the ground solemnly, with no idea of what went past him!

HIGHWAYMEN
AND THEIR HORSES

Now, I often like their horses better than I do the highwaymen. I certainly don't like Dick Turpin, the highwayman who is mentioned most often in books, and even pop songs. He was a savage, cruel man and would do anything to get people's money, even holding an old woman over a fire to get her to tell him where her money was hidden. Black Bess, his horse, however, was a great character, although she only seems to be mentioned in a Victorian novel called *Rook Wood* and not in any history books.

BLACK BESS AND DICK TURPIN

Black Bess's father was an Arabian horse brought to this country by a wealthy man, and her mother was a coal black English racer. She had an elegant little head and was built for strength more than beauty. She was so gentle, children could ride her.

Turpin's famous long ride to York began after he had mistakenly shot a highwayman friend of his called Tom King. Dick was trying hard to avoid police raids. He decided to start off from Kilburn and make his way to York, and amazingly on his way there Bess jumped the tollgate at Hornsey. When she started to get tired, Dick rubbed her with a solution of water and brandy and then swam her across the River Ouse. Then, sadly, she was just a mile out of York when she tottered and fell. There was a terrible gasp – a parting moan – a snort; her eye gazed for an instant upon her master with a dying glare; grew glassy, rayless and fixed; a shiver ran through her frame. Her heart had burst. Oh dear, brave little heroine! If only Dick could be so heroic.

BROWN MEG AND JERRY CUTTER

Brown Meg was not a handsome horse. In fact, she looked a little odd, for she had no ears!

Her owner, Jerry Cutter Lynch of Leigh-on-Sea, had some false ears made to make her look as normal as possible. In fact, he had another secret, for his name was a cover-up. He was actually called Gilbert Craddock, and he would try to give the impression that he was a London businessman. He brought a fine house that would make him look more of a gentleman, but the house needed some building work done. This meant he needed some extra money, so he became a 'gentleman of the night'.

Adding to Lynch's problems was the fact that the builders were greedy. Picking up their tankards of ale that they had been allotted did not please them. They said to the boss, 'This is not enough ale for hardworking workers like us. Have you no idea how thirsty we get?'

This made Lynch angry. He was desperate to get the work finished, so, putting his hands on his hips, he muttered, 'Well, if you get that thirsty, lap water from the horse pond.' This

caused so much laughter in the town that his new home was called Lapwater Hall.

The pond was to cause him great dismay, for not long after, he had been out on one of his nightly adventures when he was chased by the officers of the law and wounded. Nothing for it but to creep in by the back gate of Lapwater Hall, and horror of horrors, he fell in the horse pond, unable to move because of his wound. Next day it was realised who he was when they found poor Brown Meg close by, with those strange obviously waxed ears still stuck to her head!

SILVER AND STEPHEN BUNCE

He knew who was there. A commanding voice came from above Stephen Bunce.

Slyly, Bunce looked up and saw an elegant man sitting on a fine dappled silver horse, covered with marks like sixpences over its neat little body. Then, suddenly, he threw himself on the ground and lay amazed, apparently listening to something that came from the earth itself. The gentleman was amazed and moved closer to the figure on the ground but there was no reaction. 'Answer me, you fool.'

'Shh …'

'What are you hearing?'

Stephen Bunce smiled broadly. 'Fairies. I can hear fairies. It's the most beautiful sound I have ever heard. Such sweet music!'

Well, in our day and age we would laugh out loud if people spoke about fairies, imps and house elves as if they were real. But in 1707, people believed in them. The gentleman certainly could not resist it. He wanted to know more. He dismounted from his horse and gave Bunce the reins to hold, while he put his ear to the ground.

Bunce did not hesitate. He took the horse and galloped away. The gentleman, of course, heard nothing! Nothing, that is, except the thumping of hooves galloping away. Bunce

and the silver horse were well on their way to Romford.

A highwayman always knows a fine horse when he sees one. So, for that matter, does an innkeeper. The landlord of the inn recognised the silver horse as soon as he saw him. 'That's Mr Bartlett's horse.'

'So it is. So it is. Mr Bartlett has asked to offer him as a pledge. For he's asking you politely, sir, if you could lend him fifteen guineas. It's a little matter of a debt of honour at Ingstone, you understand.'

The landlord understood quickly enough. Mr Bartlett was a notorious gambler. The horse was a good bargain in the circumstances, so he handed over the fifteen guineas in a leather bag to Bunch without a protest. The highwayman had trouble keeping his face straight, but he marched away happily with his loot.

It was just as well he was not there when Mr Bartlett arrived at the inn. Sadly, we have no record of what he said when the innkeeper told him. 'There was no need to have left the horse. I would have lent you the money anyway.' Secretly the innkeeper was rather pleased. It was, after all, rather a magical horse!

FAIRY STORIES

It's rather disappointing that there are very few sightings of fairy folk in Essex unless they are what people paint themselves. Out in the country, people used to speak of brownies, who are helpful little creatures, who help in completing various country tasks; but there are also imps, who are more alarming as they are servants of the Devil, and so often used by witches.

I did find a book called *Essex: Its Forest, Folk and Folklore* written by Charlotte Mason in 1928, which now seems to have vanished from the library. But I do remember it did tell one interesting story. Apparently, Charlotte had a wizard with three imps living in her house. She warned everyone never to come into her room or she might see them.

'Do they hurt us?'

'No.' She did, in fact, catch a glimpse of them in her room, and amazingly they were the same height as the table, and even stranger they were seen walking over thistles without bending their tops.

THE BAD-TEMPERED BROWNIE

The fairy story that has lingered with me most is a tale about a brownie, a kind of house elf.

It began with Jack Smith, the squire's groom. The squire had a fine stable of hunting and racing horses. Jack longed to be able to ride them, but he did nothing but moan when he got the job, for there was little chance for himself doing any riding – nothing but sweeping the stable and polishing the tack and hauling the hay up and down the barn.

He got so terribly tired at night that he did nothing but moan to his parents, who were not at all impressed. 'You do nothing but grumble. You don't even know what hard work is. We've been farm labourers all our lives and our backs ache and ache. Wait until you are our age, and then you can grumble.'

Only Granny smiled and said, 'What you need is a brownie.'

'A brownie? Whatever is that?'

'Don't you know what a brownie is? Children nowadays know nothing. You might have heard perhaps of a hobgoblin or a boggart or a house elf, but the best little helper is a brownie.'

'But how do I get hold of one?'

'You don't know?'

'Please tell me.'

'Well, you put out bread and milk at the back door, and sure enough they'll lap it all up and immediately they'll start working for you as hard as they can, but you must be very careful not to let them see you.'

'Why not?'

Granny grinned again but said nothing more.

For the next week Jack was working as hard as he ever had, and then he tried putting out the milk and bread, and sure enough within the next week all the work was getting done without him making any effort, yet not a single sight of the brownie. Jack thought to himself, 'He must work at night. I know what I'll do. I'll wait for the full moon and see if he appears.'

Sure enough, when the full moon appeared, he looked down from the loft and saw a little man working very hard at sweeping the stable with a broom. When he saw what a curious little man he was, Jack had to smile, for the brownie had a bald head like a boiled egg, a face like a turnip, a large floppy hat, a very thin body and arms and legs no bigger than twigs. The really shocking thing was that he was not wearing a stitch of clothing except for his muddy welly boots. Jack could not help it. He was chortling with laughter at such a comic sight. The brownie looked up, and was so angry at being laughed at that he flung the broom up at the boy and its spikes fell all around him, scratching him. 'Damn you, damn you!' it screamed, and raced out into the night.

He never came back again, and Jack was now having to work so hard that he began to look like an old man with a bent back and a whiskery face. He would mutter to himself, 'I should have shown the magical gentleman more respect. I should have done what I was told.' So all that was left to him, after his hard work, was to sit night after night after night hunched up and moaning at himself for having lost such a good friend.

FUNNY MAN! FUNNY MAN!

Strangely enough, there have been very few sightings of 'little folk' (or fairies), the most famous of which was at Springfield Place near Chelmsford. News of it reached the local papers in the Second World War in the 1940s, when a rather handsome house was being used as a hostel for girls. Two of the girls staying there complained that something frightening had touched their faces while they were sleeping on the upper floor. Their story was taken seriously, and the door was kept locked afterwards. The most frequent sighting in the house had been 'of a hideous little dwarf'.

Now, this story made Mary Petrie write a letter to the press. Her family had previously lived in the house for many years. The house had always seemed peculiar, with lots of trapdoors, mysterious cupboards high up on the wall that never opened, long passages and an underground room.

Mary's relative Lucy said the most dramatic sighting was in a large bedroom which was called the Blue Room. She explained, 'My mother took my baby sister Nelly to sleep there because she was teething and we did not want to wake our father. In the middle of the night Mother was kept awake by the baby chuckles and the little voice was saying "Funny man, funny man". Of course, she did not expect to see anybody there, but to her amazement she could see a little man with his back to the fire. He was a hideous little man with his arms folded.'

Oh dear! She was terrified and back under the sheets she hid herself. He was an alarming creature. She tossed and turned and then decided to get out of her sheets to look for him, but he had gone! Baby Nelly was still chortling 'Funny man! Funny man!'

Oddly enough, people who had heard the story had lively discussions in the street. Was it a ghost? A goblin? One of the little folk? What do you think? I'll let you decide.

REMEDIES OF A WISE WOMAN

In the old days, when people were ill they did not have modern science or medicine to help them. They would go and talk to the wisest old woman in the village, who had spent her life exploring nature for cures for all types of illness. Sometimes she got it right with her experience and knowledge of herbs, which we can use today, but sometimes they were completely laughable. Look at the following list of cures the wise woman of Wormingford laid out in her book of cures.

Please don't try them yourself!

FOR EAR ACHE

Heat the kernel of the onion. Put in the ear and cover with a used stocking.

FOR A SORE THROAT

Place the halves of a heated onion in a used stocking and apply one to each side of the throat.

NOSE BLEED

Lower trousers and put in a cold cowpat.

BLEEDING

Staunch with a cobweb.

BURNS

Apply Madonna leaves steeped in brandy.

SORES

Apply a mite of mouldy cheese.

MEASLES

Drink a brew of marigold flowers followed by a draught of good ale.

WHOOPING COUGH

Skin and toast a freshly caught mouse and eat hot.

COUGHS AND COLDS

Rub back and front of chest with warm goose fat or tarrow. Give a sup of black-currant or mead.

CONGESTION OF THE LUNGS

Swallow live jakes [young frogs] to suck up the phlegm. [There was a near tragedy when the jake was found to be large for the child to swallow but the legs were sticking out and it was removed in time.]

CHILBLAINS

Beat with holly.

Back up against a hive and let out the bad blood and apply warm goose fat or tarrow.

RHEUMATISM

Back up against a hive and be well stung by the bees. A complete cure.

TALES FROM THE TOWER

Anybody who has a camera in Brightlingsea knows that the best picture to take in Brightlingsea town is that of Bateman's Tower, with either the sunset or the dawn rising behind it. The tower was built by John Bateman, who came from Staffordshire in 1871 to live with his family in Brightlingsea Hall and was given the nickname of the 'Squire', mainly for his rather grand manner.

He built the tower for his young daughter called Agnes. The tower was a more elegant version of a beach hut, and some people thought it was built for her because she had 'consumption' and needed fresh air to make her better. She was a lucky girl, for what wonderful views there must have been from there, including all the ships and boats that came up the river, and views of Mersea and the far banks of the Colne. It was a wonderful idea for a young girl and the tower must have stimulated her imagination. She grew up to be a very grand lady, which is not surprising as her mother was the sister of an earl, and Agnes married Mr D'arcy Hildyard, a lieutenant in the light infantry, and later she married a Mr Liddel.

In times of war, the tower was used as an air and sea observation tower and the upper structure was removed. Since then, a great fundraising effort by the Yacht Club, and the support and grant from the Heritage Lottery Appeal Fund, have helped make it look as splendid as possible. It is, in fact, restored very closely to the way it was constructed originally. It is now used for starting yacht races and other local events. I worked with children at Brightlingsea Junior School on stories inspired by the tower to celebrate the rebuilding. Their favourite story was 'Rapunzel' by the Brothers Grimm, of the witch who imprisoned a girl in a tower and would haul herself up to the tower's upper window by the girl's long plait. This was the story told in the film *Tangled*.

Agnes's own favourite story was the version of 'Beauty and the Beast' written by the eccentric vicar of east Mersea, Sabine Baring Gould, in his book of 'Fairy Tales'.

BEAUTY AND THE BEAST

Once upon a time there lived a rich merchant who had three daughters, and they lived in great comfort in a lovely villa in London. The loveliest of the daughters was the youngest and she was called Belle. She was so sweet tempered that it meant she never frowned nor pouted, so she always seemed charming and was happy enough to stay home in the evenings to read books. The two older daughters were lazy and wanted nothing but to go to balls and the opera.

Then, sadly, the merchant found his ships were shipwrecked and his clerk was cheating him and his firm was going bankrupt, and he had to tell his daughters.

'My darlings, I have lost my ship and my fortune so now we must move to a cottage in the country. We will have no more servants and there will be no more fine gowns and trips to the opera and to balls. So you will have to spend your time helping in the house.'

The two older girls muttered and sulked. 'We can't soil our fingers, dusting furniture or scrubbing floors. We are above such things.'

So it was Belle who would get up early in the morning – clean the house, lay and light the fire, prepare breakfast and even see there were flowers on the table. And all the time she sang like a lark and filled her head full of peaceful dreams.

As time passed, their father heard rumours that one of his ships and its cargo had been found. So he prepared to go on a journey to recover his treasure. He was so pleased that he asked his daughters what they wanted on his return from his journey.

'A pearl necklace.'

'A diamond ring.'

'A white rose.'

Amazingly, his journey went well, but he had trouble getting the pearl necklace and the diamond ring for his oldest girls, and he thought even Belle would not get her white rose, for by now winter had come and snow was falling. One day he got lost in the woods, and when riding along he saw a fine mansion with a long path lit by orange lanterns. He was cold and hungry, so he went right up to the door and banged the knocker, but there was no answer, yet the door opened slowly and he pushed it open more widely and saw a long carpeted corridor. He walked down the corridor and found a dear little sitting room with a warm flickering fire, a comfortable sofa and a table set out with a delicious meal. He could not resist it. He curled up in front of the fire and tucked into the delicious meal and soon fell asleep on velvet cushions.

In the morning, he wandered around the splendid house, which boasted a fine dining room, a cosy sitting room, and even a library and a music room, but he found no one home. So he prepared to leave, and as he stood on the patio, he suddenly saw a clump of white roses. 'Ah! My darling Belle's present,' and he plucked three lovely white roses, but to his horror, he saw through the leaves a hideous hairy face staring at him and a great body bristling with whiskers stood over him. A great roar came from the beast, and he shouted, 'Who gave you permission to gather my roses? How dare you steal my lovely roses!' and a claw shot out through the thorns and scratched the merchant's face. The merchant was beside himself with fear and told the beast all about his daughters and the presents he had promised them.

The beast's voice turned gentle. 'How lucky you are to have daughters. I am all alone in the world. I will give you the roses and if I let you go, you must promise to let one of your girls come and live with me willingly here, for I am so lonely, and I can promise she will live in the greatest comfort. If not …'

The merchant did not need to have more explained to him. He guessed what the beast might do if he was not obeyed, but even more

horrible was imagining any of the girls living with him.

At first when he got home he could not even tell the girls about the beast. He was just pleased to see their happy faces when he gave them their presents. Then, at last, he told them what the beast had wanted. The two older girls turned on Belle, and said, 'You'll have to go. It's your fault that Father met the beast. You'll have to stay with him.' Belle sighed and clung desperately to her white rose as she tried to sleep that night.

Surprisingly, she cheered up when she got to the beast's palace, for there were orange and yellow lights shining everywhere and the sweet music played. She thanked the beast for her rose and he was pleased and even allowed her to send gifts home for her sisters. Still she felt alone in the palace, but as she wandered around, she was delighted to find a music room and a library and the most lovely gardens. She even began to spend time with the beast, and found he had a beautiful deep singing voice and he knew all the names of all the flowers in the garden. She was so impressed that she made him turquoise velvet slippers embroidered with white roses with golden stamens. She was not even surprised that he asked her to marry him.

She was genuinely surprised at how gentle he was, and how learned and with such excellent manners. She hesitated about saying no, but she became very homesick and begged to be permitted to go home for a little while. The beast, reluctantly, allowed her to go for a month.

She enjoyed that month at home enormously, and almost forgot about the beast until she had the most dreadful nightmare. She dreamt the beast was dying in a cave. She was so distressed that she left home without a word to her family, murmuring 'Please don't die' to the shadow of the beast.

To her horror, when she got back, she could not find him anywhere in the palace nor in the garden, and then she remembered the grotto and its cave. There, in the gloom, she saw the hunched figure of the beast lying motionless on the floor. 'My poor beast,' she murmured, and desperately she leant over him and brushed his hairy cheek, until the fur fell away and she was looking into the face of a handsome prince. He laughed to see her look so startled. 'You have done it my darling. Your prince is a whole man again. The witch's curse is lifted. I am myself again! Now will you marry me?'

'Yes, yes ...' The whole cave echoed with their happiness, and the rocks blazed with all the colours of the rainbow as he led her out into the light and back to his wonderful palace, where they could live happily ever after.

THE KING OF COLCHESTER'S DAUGHTER

In the early days of print, cheap little books began to appear with simple stories for those who could just about read, and large woodcut drawings to illustrate them. They were sold by pedlars at fairs and usually were those tales which had been passed from person to person over the years. One of the most popular stories was 'The King of Colchester's Daughter'. It started its journey in Germany as 'The Spinning Woman by the Well', and when it first came to England it was called 'The Three Golden Heads in the Well' and was performed as a play. No doubt it was popular because of the quarrelling sisters and the spiteful stepmother.

See what you make of the two girls.

Once there was a king of Colchester who had everything a king could want – a peaceful kingdom, happy and contented subjects, a land of golden corn and plenty of oysters and good food to eat. His happiness was made complete when he married a lovely lady and they had a sweet baby daughter. Sadly, when his daughter was 15, his wife died and he was left so sad.

His courtiers nagged him to choose a new wife, if only for the sake of his motherless child. Well, he did find a new wife, and she may have been wealthy and swished around in rich clothes, but she was hideous. She had a hooked nose and a humped back. What was worse, she was grumpy with a foul temper, and she had a daughter who was just as ugly and just as bad tempered as she was. The pair of them were eaten up with envy of the king's daughter, for she was all that they were not. She carried herself with dignity, she was sweet tempered with a sunny disposition.

The palace now had a dreadful atmosphere. Nothing but squabbles, spitting tongues and spite. The king's daughter was desperately unhappy. Then, luckily, she was walking in the garden one lovely summer's evening, when the air was heavily scented with roses and lavender, when she saw the king walking on his own. At last she could speak to him openly. She ran up to him and pulled at his sleeve and looked at him so plaintively.

'Darling father, I am so sorry but I cannot live with the queen and her daughter any longer. Please may I leave home? Just give me an allowance and I am sure I can make my own way in the world.'

Her father reached down from his great height and said, 'I am so sad it has come to this. I have hated to hear you quarrel, so perhaps it is best you go, but do come back and tell me how things are with you.' He bent down and kissed her and told her to go to her stepmother to get provisions for her journey. He ought to have known better. Her stepmother only gave her a canvas bag containing bread, hard cheese and a bottle of beer! How would you feel if you were starting out in the world with such poor food and no kind words. But she went cheerfully enough; she was just so pleased to be away from the palace that she practically skipped down the road, humming a little tune to herself.

Then, by mid-afternoon, she came to a bend in the road where there was a cave, in front of which a hermit sat stroking his long white beard. (Hermits were wise old men with long white beards, who lived alone and begged for their living.)

He looked at her gently and said, 'Where are you going, my pretty?'

'I am off to seek my fortune.'

'And what have you got in that canvas bag?'

'I have bread and beer and cheese. Would you like some?'

'Thank you. I would.'

It was a poor feast, but they were both hungry and ate it all up. Then it was the hermit's turn to do her a favour. He gave her a sprig of hazel, and told that when she came to a thorny bush blocking her way she must touch its branches with the sprig three times, and say 'Hedge, I beg you to let me come through' and the hedge would let her come through. Even more strangely, she would come to a well, and out of the well would appear three golden heads and she must do what they told her.

Sure enough, only half a mile down the dusty road she came to the prickly hedge. She spoke the magic words and tapped its branches with her sprig and the hedge opened into a clearing, and there she saw the well, and from out of the well came a golden head singing the strangest song:

Wash me, comb me
Lay me down softly
And lay me on a bank to dry.
So that I look pretty
When someone passes by.

She had a silver comb in her pocket, and as gently as she could she combed the golden head and laid it on a mossy bank where primroses, violets and celandines grew. No sooner was the head on the ground when up came a second and a third head, each singing the strange song; each time, she did as it asked. Then, when they requested to be put back in the well, she obeyed them. In the depths of the well, they whispered promises to each other, determined to return her kindness.

'She is beautiful already, so I do not need to make her lovely. I shall give her the gift of charm.'

'I will make her body and breath so fragrant she will exceed the perfume of flowers.'

'She will marry the best of princes.'

Amazingly, as she reached the outskirts of a great wood, a prince emerged from the shadows with his huntsmen and hounds. One glance at her in the ray of the setting sun and he was hopelessly in love with her, so that he took her to his castle to keep her safe from the dangers of the night. There she was treated with great respect and given fine jewels and gowns. Love touched them both so quickly that a wedding was not long in coming.

It was only after the wedding that she told him she was the king of Colchester's daughter. Her husband was a little shocked.

'Your father must be missing you. We must arrange a visit immediately.' The prince was determined to make a great impression, and they rode into Colchester in a golden chariot lined with purple velvet with blood red garnets embossed in its side. The king and all the court were absolutely delighted to see them, only the stepmother and her daughter were sour-faced to see the feasting and dancing which had now broken out throughout the city.

Riddled with jealousy, the stepdaughter was determined to set out on a similar journey to meet with similar good fortune. Her mother was determined to give her all the help she could, and her daughter was given fine travelling clothes and a splendid hamper containing wild boar sandwiches, sweetmeats and the best Spanish sherry. She set off down the same road and found the hermit with the long beard sitting outside his cave.

'Where are you going in such a hurry?'

'None of your business, old man.'

'And I suppose it's none of my business as to what's in your hamper.'

'True, for I would share none of it, unless it would choke you.'

The old man muttered curses on her head. Of course, he gave her no warning about the hedge and the mysterious heads.

When in fact she did reach the hedge, she thought she saw a gap that would let her pass through, but as she pushed her way through the thorns tore at her hands and arms, and her arms bled profusely. Desperately, she looked for water to wash away the blood, and then she saw the well. When she got close to it she saw the first golden head, and it was singing that strange song:

Wash me, comb me,
Lay me down softly
And lay me down to dry
So that I look pretty
When somebody passes by.

But what a reaction! The stepsister took the bottle of sherry and knocked the head down the well, shouting, 'Take that for your washing!' This she did to the second and the third head. They sank back in the darkness, whimpering in pain, and whispered among themselves what they must do.

'I'll give her sores all over her face,' the first head vowed.

'I'll make her stink like a pig in a sty,' said the second head.

The third head said, 'And she'll marry a poor man no better than a cobbler.'

Oblivious to the changes that were happening to her, the girl set off for the nearest market town. No sooner did she arrive in the market town than people started to move away from her, for they couldn't abide to see her spotty face or be near her smell. Only a cobbler came up to her, for in his pocket he had a box of ointment that could cure sores and a bottle of spirits that could freshen mouth and body. He had been given these things as a reward for mending the shoes of a holy man. He offered her them in exchange for becoming her husband, and amazingly she was agreeable, even though at first she had been full of the fact that she was a king's stepdaughter. When her sores and bad breath had gone, she was so relieved, she snuggled happily enough into his arms.

They paid a visit to Colchester not long after their wedding. The girl's mother was so horrified that the girl had gone so low as to marry a cobbler of all people that she took her own life. Her husband inherited her wealth and gave a hundred pounds to the cobbler. They moved to a faraway village, where he became a fine shoemaker. His wife wove as fine a thread as is woven into this story.

This is, after all, a tale of love.

THE GIFT

Now, whenever I mention that I am telling Essex stories, people say, 'But you are Welsh' and so I am, yet I have lived in Essex for thirty-five years and travelled widely within the county, telling and listening to stories. Strangely enough, it was only a few days ago that I discovered that there is a Welsh connection in Essex. It is mainly with farms in the Billericay area, where you can find a lot of people with names like Evans, Jones, Thomas, Davis and even Williams living there, who it is said are descended from Welsh drovers. These drovers were sturdy men who walked for miles from Wales with their dogs and long sticks, driving their cattle and sheep from the Welsh mountains through the English midlands to the rich grazing land of Essex, where they could be fattened up for the markets of Brentwood, Romford and Harlow in Essex.

Now, when I am telling tales at Essex shows, like Tendring Agricultural Show, sometimes a farmer's child from the south comes struggling through the tent door wanting a story, and their favourite tale is about my Uncle Jack, which makes them smile, so here it is for you.

It was a wet and windy road. Uncle Jack could barely stand up against the wind. He was so fed up. It had been a dreadful day at Welshpool market, all because he had been given a dreadfully low price for his sheep and had not even got any money left over to pay for a treat for his wife. She would be furious. The rain was getting heavier, and to make matters worse he could hear the beat of a horse's hooves coming up behind him. He was terrified to look round in case it was a highwayman creeping up, ready to steal whatever he had left.

Then, suddenly, the man on the horse was by his side. He was an elegant gentleman in a large hat and a black cloak to protect him, and he was leaning down from his horse, muttering in a very posh English accent. 'My dear fellow, you look frozen stiff. Jump on the back of my horse and you can come to the manor for some warmth and good food.'

So that was it! It was the squire from the manor Plas Newydd. Uncle Jack was most relieved, and it seemed a most kind offer and he was very hungry, so he did as he was invited and jumped on the back of the horse. Off they rode through the trees dripping with rain, until they came to the clearing of the manor and saw a great white house with magnificent sash windows, with a vast number of stairs leading to the great doors.

As soon as they heard the horse and the two men arrive, down the stairs rushed the servants in their fine uniforms to attend to them. Uncle Jack found he was being led upstairs by two immaculately groomed butlers, and before he could protest he was being stripped and scrubbed for a large bath, then put in a smart outfit, including a very warm brown velvet jacket.

Then it was time for the feast. He could not believe what he was seeing. He was led into a grand hall with crowds around a great table laden with delicious food, including a great sizzling pig decorated with plump apples and fresh vegetables. At first Uncle Jack gobbled it all up, and then he looked around him and saw the grand men of the hunt and the elegant ladies in their woollen gowns decked with lace all laughing and talking and looking for entertainment. Then there was music at the piano and poems read out loud.

Then Uncle Jack realised they were all looking at him as though expecting something from him. He knew it was not going to be a song! He certainly could not sing! He could only croak. Then he realised they were all looking at him intently and banging their spoons on the table. 'Tell us a story,' they all shouted loudly. Now, I am sure that many of you have been asked to tell a story, and sure enough your mind goes blank and you can't think of anything! It was like that with Uncle Jack, and it got worse, as the squire beckoned his butlers to pick him up, take him out onto the stairs and throw him into the dark without a single word.

Luckily it had stopped raining so he was able to make his way through the trees without getting wet, and he saw the signpost which read Chapel of Sleep, so he knew which way he was going. Then he saw three old men hunched over a coffin, looking totally exhausted. They had obviously walked for miles and were trying hard to make their way to the chapel.

'Let me help you carry it,' Uncle Jack offered.

With his help the men were able to lift the coffin high, and they actually walked down the path cheerily. In fact, they began to sing the way the Welsh do at rugby matches. Soon they found the iron gates of the chapel, which opened with a creak onto rather a small graveyard. Obviously it was not used very frequently.

'Where are we putting the coffin?'

The men looked embarrassed at this and stared at a large spade, but no hole.

Uncle Jack immediately knew what was wanted. 'I'll help you,' he said in his usual helpful way. He picked up the spade and dug a grave very quickly. A spade was an easy thing for him. He had dug up enough potatoes in his time. It was simple then to slide the coffin down into that space. The men took off the lid of the coffin, and to Uncle Jack's amazement the coffin was empty!

He was about to make his usual helpful offer when he saw the men staring at him thoughtfully. 'We need a body to put in the grave.'

'Oh no! You are not putting me in the grave!' Uncle Jack declared, and swiftly picked up a great branch of hazel wood and sent the men flying into the dark. He knew now what he must do. He must make his way back to the manor and tell his story. Amazingly, he strolled up to the doors of the great hall and stood until he had everyone's attention. 'Oh my people, have I got a story to tell you,' and he told them the tale of the coffin, and he told it so well with his splendid voice and waving hands that everybody clapped and he was invited to sit at the head table, and told more stories and the people in the hall told more tales as well. It was a very exciting evening with everybody trying to outdo each other with their stories. It was almost dawn when the stories began to fade and he realised he must go home, and one of the stable grooms took him home in the family cart.

Jack did not go straight into the house, but lay down to rest in the hay of the barn. About eight o'clock his wife Myfanwy came out to feed the chickens and was amazed to find him still wearing the brown velvet jacket, and demanded to hear what had happened. She thought they should have given him more of a present.

He smiled. 'I do have a gift. I have been given the gift of how to tell a story.' She was not cross, because now he had bundles of tales to tell his children, and they say his children became wonderful storytellers, as I hope you do.

And this is some of the way we Welsh storytellers began to tell our stories. We listen wherever we travel, and share the tales we learn with everybody who comes to see us. Why not share our Essex tales all over the country!

A Big Thank You

And this storyteller wants to thank all the people who helped her put the stories together.

I want to thank my dear and loving partner, Peter Fowler, who takes me everywhere and listens to all my tales with such gentle understanding.

I want to thank Margaret Hawkins, who understands computers and me!

I want to thank my good friends Katrina James and Margaret Notley, for giving me such support when I was struggling hard.

I want to thank all my listeners for listening so hard.

I want to thank The History Press, and especially Nicola Guy, for supporting me and oral storytelling.

Society *for* Storytelling

Since 1993, the Society for Storytelling has championed the art of oral storytelling and the benefits it can provide – such as improving memory more than rote learning, promoting healing by stimulating the release of neuropeptides, or simply great entertainment! Storytellers, enthusiasts and academics support and are supported by this registered charity to ensure the art is nurtured and developed throughout the UK.

Many activities of the Society are available to all, such as locating storytellers on the Society website, taking part in our annual National Storytelling Week at the start of every February, purchasing our quarterly magazine *Storylines*, or attending our Annual Gathering – a chance to revel in engaging performances, inspiring workshops, and the company of like-minded people.

You can also become a member of the Society to support the work we do. In return, you receive free access to *Storylines*, discounted tickets to the Annual Gathering and other storytelling events, the opportunity to join our mentorship scheme for new storytellers, and more. Among our great deals for members is a 30% discount off titles in the *Folk Tales* series from The History Press website.

For more information, including how to join, please visit

www.sfs.org.uk